Dear Parents and Educators,

Welcome to Penguin Young Readers! As parents and educators, you know that each child develops at his or her own pace—in terms of speech, critical thinking, and, of course, reading. Penguin Young Readers recognizes this fact. As a result, each Penguin Young Readers book is assigned a traditional easy-to-read level (1–4) as well as a Guided Reading Level (A–P). Both of these systems will help you choose the right book for your child. Please refer to the back of each book for specific leveling information. Penguin Young Readers features esteemed authors and illustrators, stories about favorite characters, fascinating nonfiction, and more!

Family Reunion

LEVEL 3

GUIDED READING LEVEL **M**

This book is perfect for a **Transitional Reader** who:

- can read multisyllable and compound words;
- can read words with prefixes and suffixes;
- is able to identify story elements (beginning, middle, end, plot, setting, characters, problem, solution); and
- can understand different points of view.

Here are some **activities** you can do during and after reading this book:
- Adding -ing to Words: There are many rules when adding -ing to words: If a word ends with a vowel and a consonant, repeat the consonant before adding -ing: hum/humming. If a word ends with an e, delete it before adding -ing: skate/skating. If a word ends with two vowels and then a consonant, just add -ing: clean/cleaning. If a word ends with a y, just add -ing: say/saying. Find the -ing words in this story. On a separate sheet of paper, write the -ing word and the root word next to it. Then identify the rule above that applies to each word.
- Creative Writing: Pretend you are going to a family reunion. Pick a relative you might see and write down a list of adjectives that describe him or her.

Remember, sharing the love of reading with a child is the best gift you can give!

—Bonnie Bader, EdM
  Penguin Young Readers program

*Penguin Young Readers are leveled by independent reviewers applying the standards developed by Irene Fountas and Gay Su Pinnell in *Matching Books to Readers: Using Leveled Books in Guided Reading*, Heinemann, 1999.

To David who always helps with
the math homework!—BB

For Glenna and Ian—MGC

Penguin Young Readers
Published by the Penguin Group
Penguin Group (USA) Inc., 375 Hudson Street, New York, New York 10014, USA
Penguin Group (Canada), 90 Eglinton Avenue East, Suite 700, Toronto, Ontario M4P 2Y3, Canada
(a division of Pearson Penguin Canada Inc.)
Penguin Books Ltd, 80 Strand, London WC2R 0RL, England
Penguin Ireland, 25 St Stephen's Green, Dublin 2, Ireland (a division of Penguin Books Ltd)
Penguin Group (Australia), 707 Collins Street, Melbourne, Victoria 3008, Australia
(a division of Pearson Australia Group Pty Ltd)
Penguin Books India Pvt Ltd, 11 Community Centre, Panchsheel Park, New Delhi–110 017, India
Penguin Group (NZ), 67 Apollo Drive, Rosedale, Auckland 0632, New Zealand
(a division of Pearson New Zealand Ltd)
Penguin Books (South Africa), Rosebank Office Park, 181 Jan Smuts Avenue,
Parktown North 2193, South Africa
Penguin China, B7 Jiaming Center, 27 East Third Ring Road North,
Chaoyang District, Beijing 100020, China

Penguin Books Ltd, Registered Offices: 80 Strand, London WC2R 0RL, England

Text copyright © 2003 by Bonnie Bader. Illustrations copyright © 2003 by Mernie Gallagher Cole. All rights reserved. First published in 2003 under the title *Graphs* by Grosset & Dunlap, an imprint of Penguin Group (USA) Inc. Published in 2013 by Penguin Young Readers, an imprint of Penguin Group (USA) Inc., 345 Hudson Street, New York, New York 10014. Manufactured in China.

Library of Congress Control Number: 2003005966

ISBN 978-0-448-42896-3   10 9 8 7 6 5 4 3 2 1

FAMILY REUNION

Formerly titled *Graphs*

by Bonnie Bader
illustrated by Mernie Gallagher Cole

Penguin Young Readers
An Imprint of Penguin Group (USA) Inc.

"Time to get up!" my mom called.
I looked at the clock. It read 7:00.
There must be some mistake, I
thought. It was Saturday morning.
I had no school today.

"Come on, Gary," my mom said.

I turned over. I pulled the pillow over my head.

"Get out of bed. Now."

She sounded serious. I pulled the pillow off my face. I opened one eye.

"Why so early?" I whispered.

"Don't you remember?" my mom said. "Today's our family reunion."

"Umph!" I muttered. I pulled the covers over my head.

"Let's go," my mom said. She pulled the covers off my head. "We're leaving in half an hour."

I knew I had to think fast. There was no way I was going to suffer through another Graff Family Reunion.

"I-I have to stay home and clean out my closet," I said.

"Nice try," my mom said with a smile. "I cleaned out your closet last week."

"Um, um, I have to stay home and do laundry," I said.

Mom shook her head. She held out a clean pair of shorts and a T-shirt for me to wear.

"I-I have to stay home and do my math homework," I said.

Mom was quiet. It looked like she was thinking about it. Maybe that excuse would work.

"You can bring your math homework with you," my mom told me. "I'm sure Aunt Molly will have a table you can use to work on."

Rats! I guess I had no choice but to go.

After a very long car ride, we finally arrived at Aunt Molly Graff's house. Most of the Graff family was already there.

"Oh, look how much you have grown!" Aunt Molly said as she gave my right cheek a big pinch.

"Oh, you look just like your father!"
Aunt Sadie said as she gave my left
cheek an even bigger pinch.

"Oh, no, I think you look just
like your mother!" Aunt Jenny said.
I ducked before she could find
something else to pinch.

There was no way I was going to
stand around getting pinched all day.
"Um, Mom," I said. "Homework time."
She gave me a nod. I made my move.

I went inside to find an empty room. Uncle Stanley was sleeping in the family room. Too noisy.

My cousins were playing dolls in the living room. Too girly.

Little Allie was getting her diaper changed in the bedroom. Too stinky.

I went outside
again. Maybe I could
find a tree to sit under.
Yes! I found a tree.
There was shade. And
there was no one around.

I sat down and
pulled out my
math book.

I had to make at least three different graphs. A bar graph. A line graph. A pie graph.

What in the world was I going to graph? I lay back on the grass to think.

Just then I heard voices. It sounded like Aunt Molly and Aunt Sadie were arguing. I opened one eye to spy.

"It's going to be at least one hundred degrees today!" Aunt Molly said. "All my food will spoil!"

"Oh, Molly, you always worry. I don't think we'll break ninety degrees today," Aunt Sadie said.

"Ninety will be just as bad!" Aunt Molly shouted. "Look at the time. It's only eleven o'clock. And it's already eighty-eight degrees. By noon it'll be ninety-two for sure!" And with that, Aunt Molly stormed away.

I bolted up. I had just gotten an idea for my first graph. I would chart the temperature and the time.

I got to work.

I had just started plotting my graph when Aunt Sadie spotted me.

"Gary!" she cried. "Why are you sitting there all by yourself? Go join the rest of the family!"

"But, I . . ." I began.

"No buts," Aunt Sadie said. "This
is a party. Now go join the fun.
Shoo! Shoo!"

I got going.

I didn't get very far before Aunt Molly caught me. She did not look happy.

"Gary," she said. "It's time to eat."

I looked at my watch. It was not lunchtime.

"But it's too early for lunch," I said.

"Well, we all have to start eating now," Aunt Molly said. "It's going to be a hot one today, and I don't want my food to spoil."

I did not want to argue with her.

Then she grabbed me. *Oh no,* I

thought. *Here comes another pinch.*

Instead of a pinch, Aunt Molly

just pulled me close and whispered

in my ear, "Be sure to try some of

my homemade potato salad. It's

better than Aunt Sadie's coleslaw.

She bought it at the store!"

I wasn't hungry. But I had another idea. When no one was looking, I slipped under the salad table. I pulled out some paper. And some sharpened pencils. I waited. And I watched.

Five aunts took the potato salad. So did my mom.

Six cousins took the macaroni salad. So did three uncles. And my dad.

And two aunts, four cousins, and eight uncles piled their plates with coleslaw. My grandma and grandpa took some, too.

I waited awhile longer. But there were no more takers.

My bar graph was done. The coleslaw was the clear favorite.

I would make sure not to tell Aunt Molly.

My stomach started to growl.

I looked at my watch. It was 1:00.

My stomach would have to wait.

I raced over to the thermometer.

It read 93 degrees.

I marked the temperature on my graph.

I walked over to the food tables.
I piled my plate high. I picked up a
knife and a fork. But there weren't
any napkins.

I looked around at my family. A few people had napkins. But most didn't. I got another idea for a graph.

I quickly ate my lunch.
Then I started to walk
around with my notebook.
I counted 10 people
using napkins.

I counted 13
people using their
sleeves.

And I counted 22
people using the back
of their hands!

Yuck!

But at least

another graph

was done!

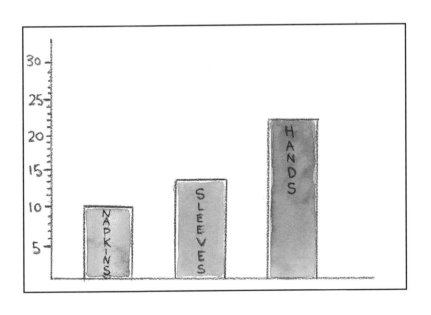

29

As I looked around for something else to do, a girl came up to me.

She had red hair and blue eyes.

"Hi!" she said. "I'm Becky. I think we're related."

"Of course we are," I told her. "That's why we're all here."

"Do you want to play?" Becky asked me.

I looked at my watch. It was 2:00.

"Sorry," I told her. "I have things to do."

I walked over to the thermometer.

It read 95 degrees.

I made a mark on my graph.

When I was done, I looked up. Becky was standing there. A boy was standing next to her. He looked just like her. Same hair. Same eyes. Same height.

"This is my brother, Bobby," Becky told me. "We're twins."

"I can see that," I said.

"Want to play?" Bobby asked.

"Sorry," I said. "I have work to do."

I started to walk away.

Becky and Bobby followed me.

"What kind of work?" Becky

wanted to know.

I told them about my math homework. I thought they would be bored by it and leave me alone.

I was wrong.

"Cool!" said Becky.

"We love math!" said Bobby. "Can
we help? This reunion is pretty boring."

"I guess," I said. "But only if you can think of something to graph."

"How about hair color?" Becky asked. "I think there are more redheads here than anything else."

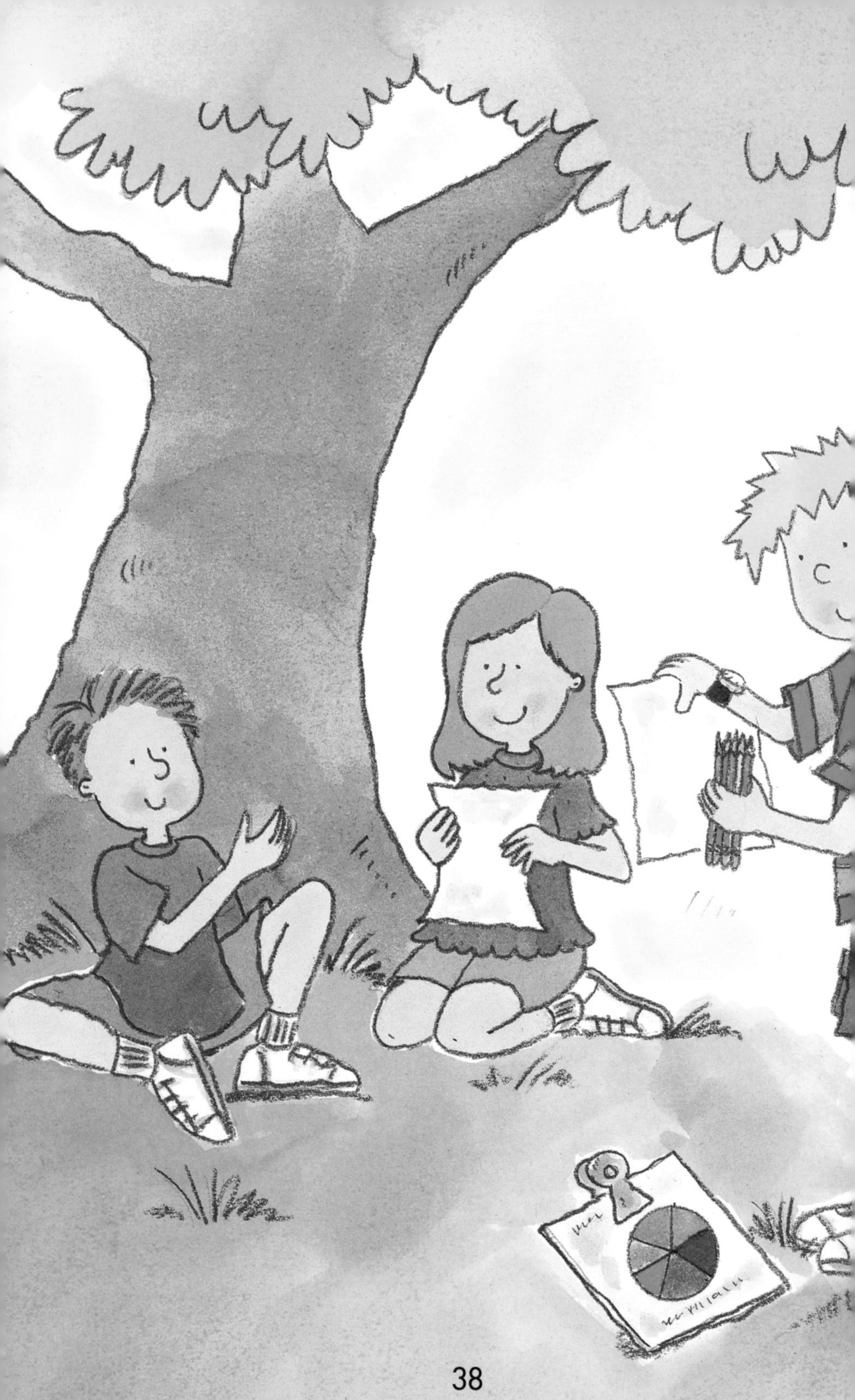

I thought a minute.

Then I handed Becky and Bobby some paper.

"Okay," I said. "Becky, you count the people with red hair. Bobby, you do brown. I'll do blond and other."

"Other?" Becky and Bobby said together.

"You'll see," I said with a smile. "Now, shoo! Shoo!"

Yikes! I was starting to sound like Aunt Sadie!

We met up a little while later.

Bobby had counted people with brown hair.

Becky had counted people with red hair.

And I had counted people with blond hair.

And people with no hair.

"Oh, so that was the other!" Bobby said.

"I thought the other was going to be gray hair," Becky said.

I looked around. There were no people with gray hair. "That's strange," I said. "There are some old people here, but no one has gray hair."

Blond IIII IIII.
Bald IIII
Brown IIII IIII
Red IIII IIII IIII

"You're right," Bobby said.

"Maybe if we get up real close to them we can find out their real hair colors," Becky suggested.

Just then, two more kids walked up to us.

"Hi! I'm Sally, and this is my brother Sammy. What are you guys doing?"

I filled them in on my math project.

"Cool," said Sally.

"Supercool," said Sammy.

Cool. That reminded me that I had to check the temperature.

I excused myself and made another mark on my graph.

As I was heading
back, my cousins
were nowhere in
sight.

I looked around.
Bobby was giving
Aunt Jenny a kiss.

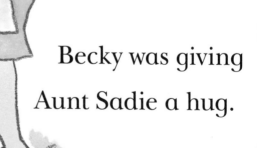

Becky was giving
Aunt Sadie a hug.

Sally was sitting
on Uncle Max's lap.
And Sammy was
letting Aunt Molly
give him a pinch.

We now had four gray-haired people.
I fixed my data. My graphs were done.

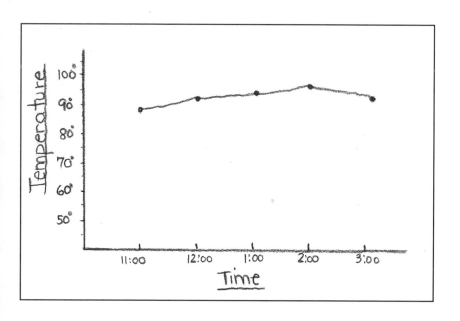

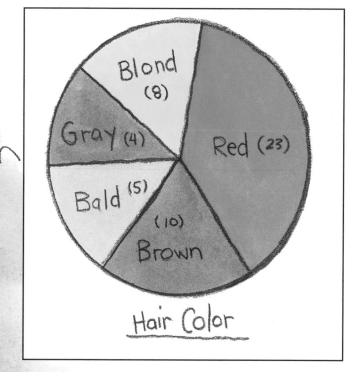

Hair Color

"Time to go home, Gary!" my mom called.

"So soon?" I asked.

My mom gave me a strange look. "You mean you had fun?" she asked.

I smiled. I said good-bye to my cousins. We made plans to see one another soon. This family reunion wasn't so bad after all.

Plus, I got my math homework done!